Dear Juliana,
Stay the kind and
gentle person that you are.
Keep your chin up and
stay strong. I care about you!
With love,
Miss Kendra

The Legend of Miss Kendra

illustrated by
Tanya Leonello

Dedicated to all Miss Kendras
wherever you are

Who notice, and ask, and listen
to our children

Each and every day
Each and every one!

Printed in the USA.

Rev. date: 10/24/2017

1-888-795-4274
www.Xlibris.com
Orders@Xlibris.com

The
Legend
of Miss
Kendra

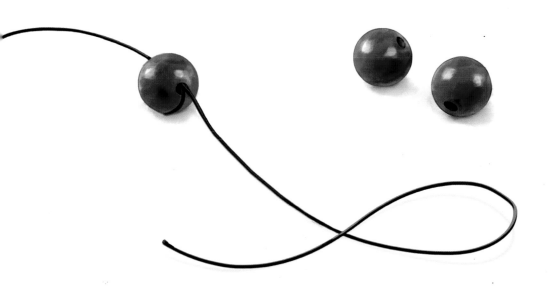

Once upon a time there was a woman
named Miss Kendra. We think she lived
near here but no one is really sure.

When she was a young woman she gave birth to a child, who made her very happy. She loved the child more than anything in her life. They did many things together.

Sadly, this child died around the age of ten. Some say the child died of an illness; some say the child was lost; or was accidentally hurt. No one is sure.

Miss Kendra was told by the doctors that she could not have another child, so she was very sad. Only her loving dog made her feel better. He went with her everywhere and kept his eye on her, making sure she was safe.

One day, when Miss Kendra was walking to work in the morning, she passed by a school, and she stopped for awhile to look at the students getting off their buses and running into the school.

She thought about her own child being one of these students and this made her feel better. "If only every child was safe," she thought to herself. If only her own child had been safe.

So Miss Kendra decided to help out at the school and every morning she was allowed to stand at the door to greet the students. Sometimes she brought cookies, and she always had a smile. Miss Kendra worried about every child who got off those buses. She looked every child in the eye to see if they were okay. She began asking the children, "Good morning, how are you doing, are you okay?" The students liked being asked, even when they were feeling well.

As the days went on, Miss Kendra began to ask more questions, like "has anyone hurt you?" and "have you been left alone?" and "is anyone at home sick?" Even when they said, "I'm fine," Miss Kendra was able to see when a student was upset about something.

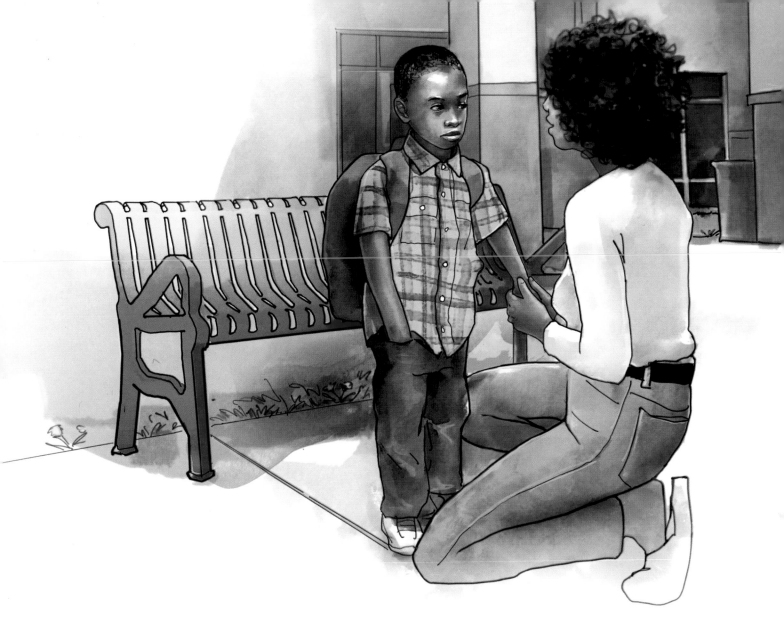

Over time Miss Kendra had certain questions that seemed just right. Most students just smiled and passed by, but some answered and some said, "Yes," that bad things had happened.

Sometimes children said that they had been punched or kicked.

Sometimes that they had been left alone or not given food for a long time.

Sometimes they had been bullied
or told they were no good.

Sometimes they had been scared
by gunshots in the neighborhood.

Sometimes they had been touched in their private parts.

Sometimes they had seen their family yell and hurt each other.

Miss Kendra felt badly for these students, but she didn't know what to do to make them feel better. One day she had an idea and so when any student said, "yes" to one of her questions, she handed them a bright red wooden bead, saying, "This is for your strength!" squeezing it into their small hands. They liked this very much because it made them feel that someone cared, that someone was watching out for them.

Soon everyone looked forward to Miss Kendra greeting them in the morning, and the parents especially appreciated that someone was keeping an eye on their children and making sure they were safe.

As the years went by, the special questions Miss Kendra asked became known as "Miss Kendra's List," and some of the students never forgot them. When they grew up some of them became teachers and they too asked their students if they were okay, if they were being hurt.

They put together her list and placed it on the wall in their classrooms so everyone could remember them.

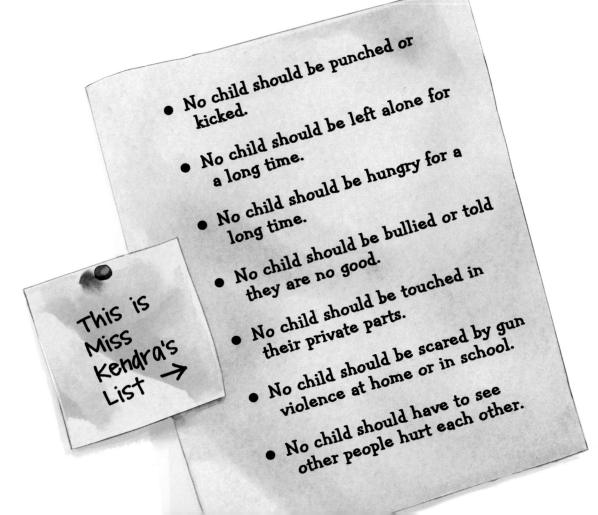

Because →

- It makes a child not care about school.

- It makes a child feel sad or scared or lonely.

- It makes a child feel angry and want to fight too much.

- It makes a child feel like not trying hard or giving up.

- It makes a child worry a lot about their family.

This is what Miss Kendra says

WHAT DO YOU SAY?

One day, some students had a great idea. They asked their teacher if they could write a letter to Miss Kendra, to tell her about their worries. The teacher thought that was a wonderful idea and after some time, found Miss Kendra, who said, "Of course I would love to get your students' letters!"

And so the letters came, full of all the worries of students! But then after a short while, something amazing happened!

The students who wrote to Miss Kendra got a letter back from her, each and every one! They were so happy! Miss Kendra had read their letters!

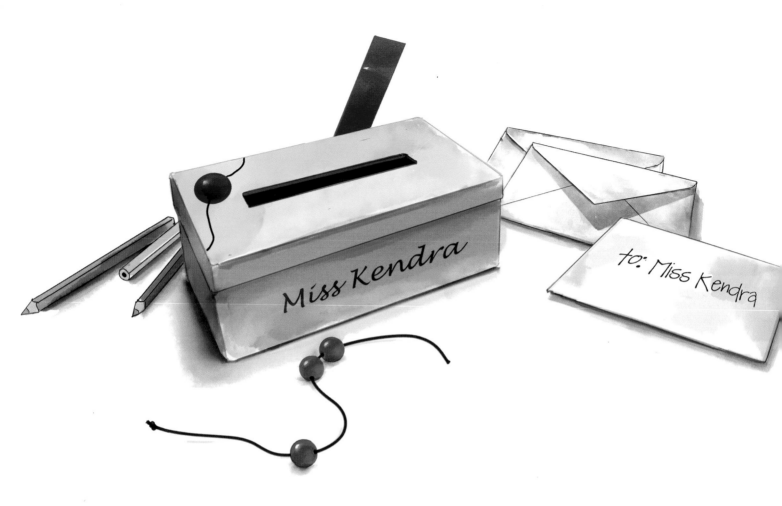

The teachers were also happy and they put out a special Miss Kendra mailbox in their classrooms for all the letters.

And the teachers gave students who had gone through hard times a red wooden bead, just like Miss Kendra, squeezing it into their hands.

This made them feel very happy, so happy the students would sing a little song:

"Miss Kendra lost her only child,
And cannot lose another.
She lived through hard times,
But that has made her stronger.
I don't have to feel sad or scared or lonely
Because Miss Kendra cares for me!"

And their days were spent having fun and playing outdoors, rather than worrying or being upset.

Sometimes when the children found a bright red bead
in their hand, or pocket, or backpack, they remembered how
strong they were to live through the hard times…that someone
cared, that someone was watching out for them. And that
thought will always make Miss Kendra happy, wherever she is!

And remember that no matter where you are, no matter how much you are worried about yourself or your family, know that Miss Kendra and all her friends are nearby, and that they care for you and want you to be safe.